There once was a goat named Tommy,
born not too long ago.

His parents said he could do anything,
but nobody knew just how far he'd go.

When he was young, the others would call him small and slow. He took it all in stride and kept practicing how to throw.

As Tommy got older, his arm strength began to grow. The others took notice, but nobody thought Tommy would go pro.

They continued to question his skills, but it didn't hurt his ego.

Tommy knew he had worked hard and had a goal of where he'd go.

When he got drafted, it took the animals by surprise.

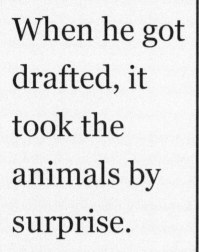

His team drafted him after 198 others, and even they didn't realize...

The highs that Tommy would lead
them to, just like he visualized.

You see, Tommy knew he'd be great, if he only got his shot.

So when Drew
went out with an
injury,

Tommy took his spot!

He led the team to greatness, and they ended the season on top.

With a Super Bowl victory, Tommy had
already accomplished a lot.

And that's where the story ends...

At least, that's what
the doubters thought...

But Tommy continued to go on a roll, and led his team to multiple Super Bowls.

In 2015, when his team was down,

Tommy helped turn the game around.

In 2017, when they said the game was a wrap,

Tommy led his team to the biggest comeback.

With five Super Bowl trophies to his name, Tommy has made his case for the Hall of Fame.

Now there's nothing left
for Tommy to do, except
smile at the doubters
and say, "I told you!"

And yes, the critics continue to whine, but Tommy doesn't bother, because he's the **Greatest Of All Time!!**

CPSIA information can be obtained
at www.ICGtesting.com
Printed in the USA
LVHW071110110219
607106LV00008B/468/P

9 781641 367035